ELEPHANT'S BIG SOLO

SARAH KURPIEL

GREENWILLOW BOOKS

An Imprint of HarperCollinsPublishers

THIS NOTEBOOK BELONGS TO

Elephant

The illustrations were created digitally.
The text type is Serifa BT.

Library of Congress Cataloging-in-Publication Data

Names: Kurpiel, Sarah, author.
Title: Elephant's big solo / written and illustrated by Sarah Kurpiel.
Description: First edition. | New York : Greenwillow Books, 2022. |
  Audience: Ages 4–8 | Audience: Grades K–1 | Summary: "Elephant's
  reluctance to perform at the class recital leads her to make new
  discoveries about her talents"— Provided by publisher.
Identifiers: LCCN 2021055299 | ISBN 9780063093201 (hardcover)
Subjects: CYAC: Self-confidence—Fiction. | Self-realization—Fiction. |
  Friendship—Fiction. | LCGFT: Animal fiction. | Picture books.
Classification: LCC PZ7.1.K87 El 2022 | DDC [E]—dc23
LC record available at https://lccn.loc.gov/2021055299
  22 23 24 25 26 RTLO 10 9 8 7 6 5 4 3 2 1
First Edition

 Greenwillow Books

For anyone
searching for their
own way to shine

Elephant had a way of standing out,
even when she'd rather not.

That's why her favorite class was music,
where she never stood alone.
But today, Ms. Gator had an announcement.

"This year, you each get to perform a solo!
Doesn't that sound wonderful?"

Everyone signed up—

except Elephant. *Perform on stage? In front of an audience? Alone?* That did not sound wonderful to her.

But the next day, Ms. Gator pulled
Elephant aside.

Sign Up
Snake
Pigeon   Pig
Hedgehog
★ ★
HARE ★
frog
ZEBRA
Turtle
FLAMINGO   TIGER
Elephant   mice

"I've added your name, in case you change
your mind. A solo is nothing to worry about.
Have *fun* with it! You'll do great."

That's what people who never get
nervous like to say, thought Elephant.

"It's just a small recital," said Tiger.
"It feels big to me," said Elephant.

"It's our moment to shine!" said Hare.
"There's more than one way to shine,"
said Elephant. "At least I hope there is."

"Sometimes we need to push
   ourselves," said Grandpa.
"I do push myself," said Elephant.
"I'm even writing a song."

"All I'm saying," said Grandpa,
"is you deserve to be heard."

I hear me, thought Elephant.

I guess that doesn't count.

Every day, Elephant tried to focus on her solo.
But she had trouble concentrating in class.

Instead, she helped her friends.

At home, Elephant practiced practiced practiced until, finally, she knew her solo by heart. But even that didn't ease her mind.

It only wore her out.

Maybe I don't deserve to be heard, she thought.

Far too soon, it was time for rehearsal.
"One week till showtime!" sang Ms. Gator.
"First up, Turtle!"

Elephant worried. Just imagining herself on stage made her heart thump, her trunk twist, and her stomach ache. *Maybe Ms. Gator will forget to call my name,* she hoped.

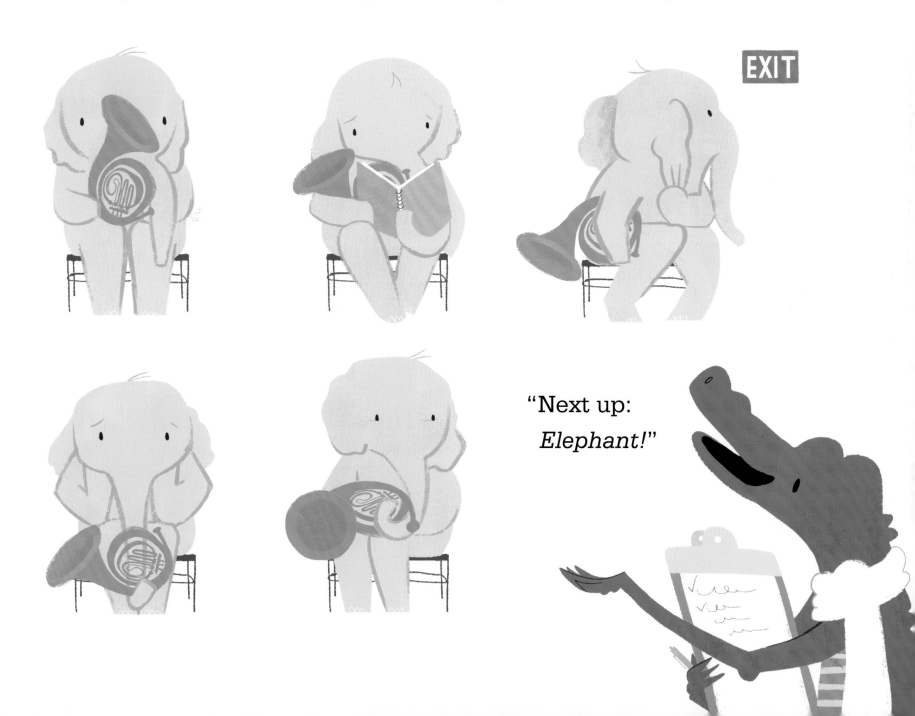

EXIT

"Next up: *Elephant!*"

Elephant did not like this class anymore. She did not like the French horn. She did not like music. She did not even like her favorite teacher.

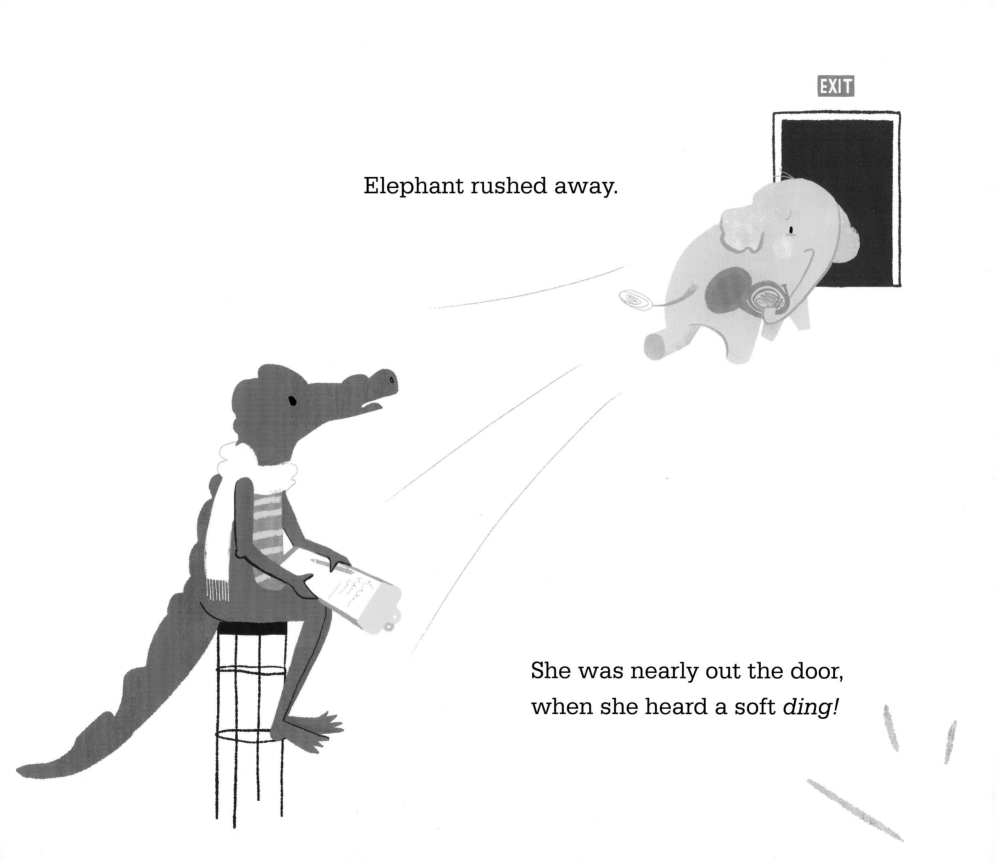

Elephant rushed away.

She was nearly out the door,
when she heard a soft *ding!*

"I'll play with you," called Tiger.

"Me too!" said Hare.

"So will I," said Snake.

Everyone wanted to help.
That gave Elephant a brave idea.

With a shaky trunk, she held up her solo.

"I wrote this song myself."

Elephant had never shared *that* before.

"Maybe I could teach it to you."

Elephant found

her own way to shine.

And when the class performed her solo together,

it felt wonderful to be heard.